NICK JR.
GO DIEGO GO!

The Rainforest Race

adapted by Lara Bergen

based on the teleplay by Rosemary Contreras

illustrated by Corey Wolfe and Art Mawhinney

SCHOLASTIC INC.

New York Toronto London Auckland Sydney
Mexico City New Delhi Hong Kong Buenos Aires

Hi, I am  !
DIEGO

Today is the Rainforest Race!

I love races!

Do you?

There are animal teams
from all over the rainforest.
There is a  team,
SPECTACLED BEAR
a team,
HOWLER MONKEY
and a team.
PUMA

The winner of the race will get a big, blue  .

RIBBON

wants to be

ARMADILLO

in the race too.

But she does not have

a team.

I know.

I will join her team!

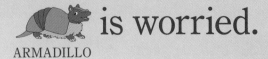 is worried.

ARMADILLO

The other animals are bigger.

But  has a strong shell.

ARMADILLO

She has sharp claws.

And she can roll into a ball.

BALL

The other animals cannot

do that!

It is time to start the race!

We need to go to the

shaky  NUT TREES,

the muddy MUD slide,

and the big MOUNTAIN.

Ready, set, go!

Here are the shaky 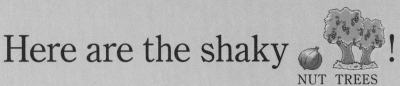!

The 🥥 are slowing

NUTS

the big animals down.

But  has a strong shell.
ARMADILLO

The  do not stop her.
NUTS

Go, , go!
ARMADILLO

Now we are at

the muddy  slide.

MUD

The PUMAS , the SPECTACLED BEARS ,

and the HOWLER MONKEYS slide down.

Oh, no!

 ARMADILLO cannot slide.

Her short legs are stuck

in the MUD.

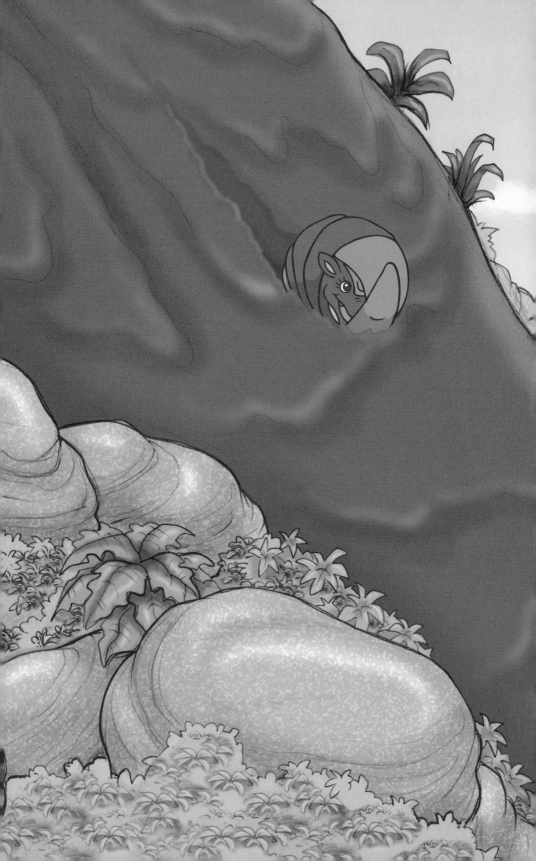

But  can roll into a ⬤.
ARMADILLO BALL

🦔 can roll down
ARMADILLO

the muddy 🟤 slide.
MUD

Roll, 🦔, roll!
ARMADILLO

We made it to the big  .

MOUNTAIN

The other teams are

at the top.

ARMADILLO is at the bottom.

Her legs are too short.

It is hard for her

to climb the ▲.
MOUNTAIN

I know how to get to the other side of the  !
MOUNTAIN

ARMADILLO has sharp claws.

She can dig a TUNNEL !

Dig, , dig!

ARMADILLO

We are almost there!

We made it to the  !
FINISH LINE

Here come the other animals.

They can run fast.

But ARMADILLO can roll faster.

Roll,  , roll!
ARMADILLO

Roll across the  .
FINISH LINE

We did it!

We won the Rainforest Race!

Everyone gets a big 🎀 .
RIBBON

Hooray for teamwork!